THIS BOOK BELONGS TO:

_____

SANTA CLAUS
and the THREE BEARS

By Maria Modugno
Illustrated by Brooke Dyer and Jane Dyer

HARPER
An Imprint of HarperCollinsPublishers

Santa Claus and the Three Bears

Text copyright © 2013 by Maria Modugno

Illustrations copyright © 2013 by Brooke Dyer and Jane Dyer

Library of Congress Cataloging-in-Publication Data is available.

ISBN 978-0-06-170023-1

The artists used Da Vinci Paint Co. watercolors and

M. Graham & Co. artists' gouache on Arches 140 lb. hot press paper.

Typography by Rachel Zegar

13 14 15 16 17 LP 10 9 8 7 6 5 4 3 2

❖

First Edition

For D.B.B. Always.
—M.M.

For Clementine, Blue, and
Violet—with love.
—J.D. & B.D.

ONCE UPON A TIME, there were three bears: a great big Papa Bear, a middle-size Mama Bear, and a wee little Baby Bear. It was Christmas Eve, and they were busy decorating their house with holly and berries and icicles.

Papa Bear was bringing in a tree from the forest,
Mama Bear was preparing Christmas pudding,

and Baby Bear was busy getting in the way.
Even though he was a baby, he was still pretty big.

The stockings were hung and the tree was decorated
when Mama Bear called everyone to dinner. She put the
Christmas pudding in a great big bowl for Papa Bear, she
put some in a middle-size bowl for herself, and she put
some in a wee little bowl for Baby Bear. But when they
sat down to eat, the pudding was too hot.

"Let's take a walk while the pudding cools," said Papa Bear.
"We can see all the Christmas lights," said Mama Bear.
"I'm coming too," said Baby Bear, and the three bears set out together.

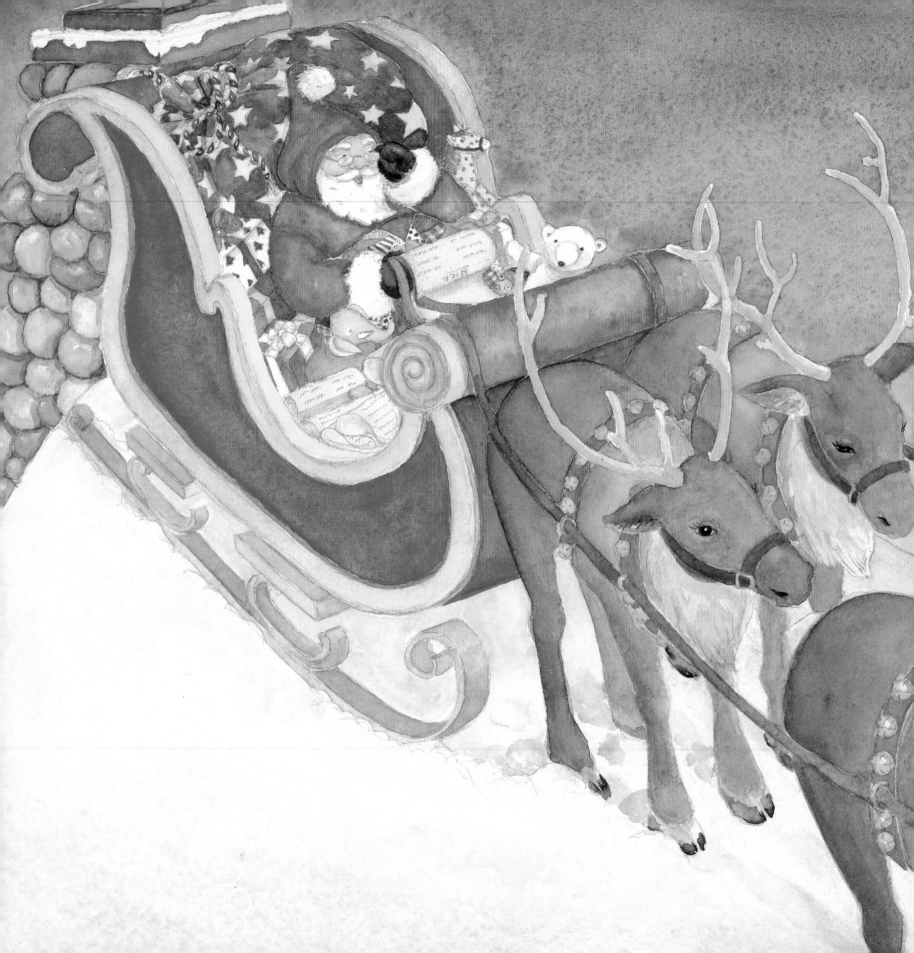

Meanwhile, Santa had finished delivering presents to everyone in the Southern Hemisphere, and he was halfway through the northern part of the world when his sleigh landed on the roof of the three bears' house. All three bears were on Santa's list for Christmas presents.

Their house shook and rumbled as Santa Claus tumbled down the chimney. Santa stood up and brushed himself off. He looked around and saw the pudding on the table. After eating milk and cookies all night, the pudding looked tasty and warm.

"Christmas pudding! What a splendid idea!" Santa exclaimed, and took a spoonful from the great big bowl.

"This pudding is too hot!" he said, and tasted the pudding in the middle-size bowl. "This pudding is too cold!"

He decided to move on to the
pudding in the wee little bowl.
"This pudding is just right," he
said, and he ate it all up!

BABY

Then Santa Claus sat down in
Papa Bear's chair.
  "This chair is too hard," he said.

He sat down in Mama Bear's chair.
"This chair is too soft."

And then he sat down in Baby Bear's chair, and it was neither too hard nor too soft, but just right. So then Santa bounced up and down a little bit, just to get comfortable, and the chair broke and Santa landed—*boom!*—on the floor.

Santa picked himself up and decided he needed a little nap before continuing on his way. He took his sack and went upstairs, where he found three beds in a row. Santa Claus lay down on the bed of the Papa Bear and said, "This bed is too high!" and he got up and tried the bed of the Mama Bear.

"Whoa! This bed is too low!" he said as he rolled off onto the floor.

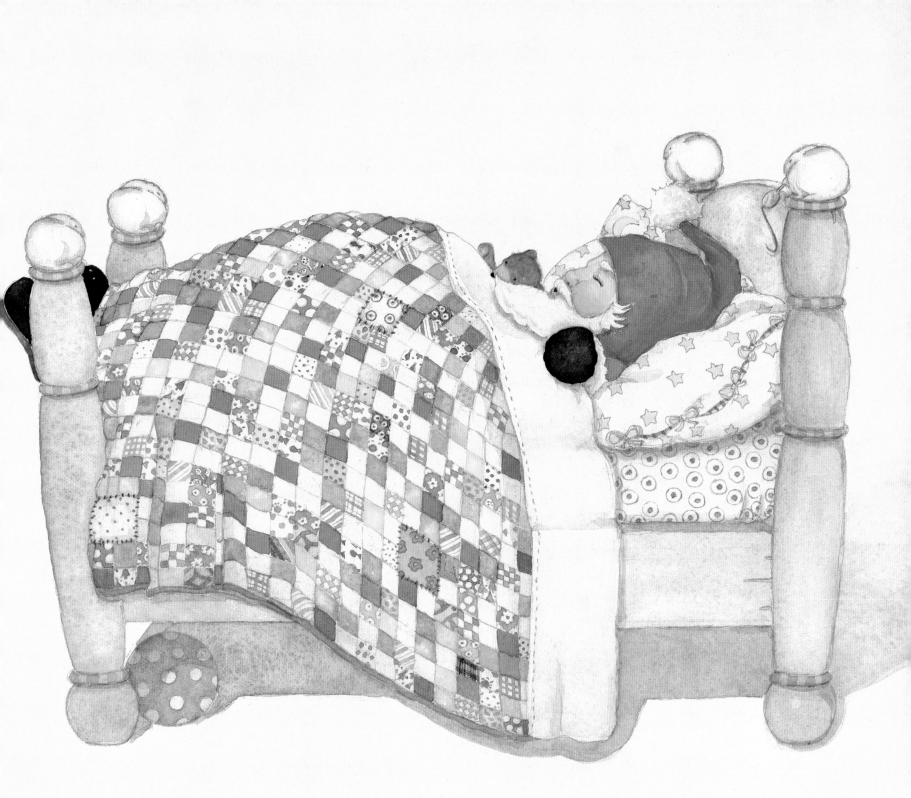

Last of all, Santa Claus tried the wee little bed of the
Baby Bear, and it was just right. So he snuggled under
the covers and fell fast asleep.

By this time, the three bears were returning home.

"SOMEBODY HAS BEEN EATING MY PUDDING!"

said Papa Bear in his great big voice.

"SOMEBODY HAS BEEN EATING MY PUDDING!"

said Mama Bear in her middle-size voice.

"SOMEBODY HAS BEEN EATING MY PUDDING," said Baby Bear in his wee little voice, "AND HAS EATEN IT ALL UP!"

The three bears looked around and saw that someone had indeed been there.

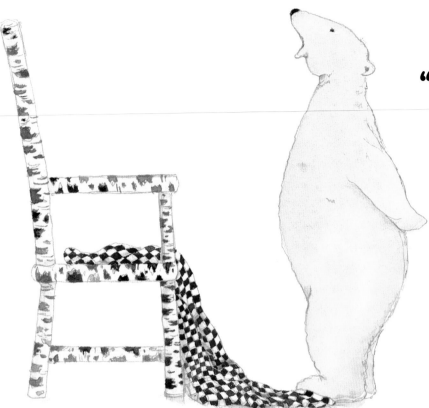

"SOMEBODY HAS BEEN SITTING IN MY CHAIR!"

said Papa Bear in his great big voice.

"SOMEBODY HAS BEEN SITTING IN MY CHAIR!"

said Mama Bear in her middle-size voice.

"SOMEBODY HAS BEEN SITTING IN MY CHAIR," said Baby
Bear in his wee little voice, "AND HAS BROKEN IT TO PIECES!"

The three bears ran upstairs to see if they
could find the mysterious visitor.

**"SOMEBODY HAS BEEN
SLEEPING IN MY BED!"**
said Papa Bear in his great big voice.

**"SOMEBODY HAS BEEN
SLEEPING IN MY BED!"**
said Mama Bear in her middle-size voice.

"SOMEBODY IS SLEEPING IN MY BED," said Baby Bear in his wee little voice, "AND WHO COULD IT BE?"

The three bears looked at Baby Bear's bed. They saw lots of white hair, a red jacket covered with soot, and, sticking out from the bottom of the blanket, two black boots.

"It's Santa Claus!" cried Baby Bear.

"Oh no! And ho, ho, ho!" said Santa Claus. "Promise you won't tell anyone you saw me? Please?" Then Santa reached into his sack and pulled out a great big present for Baby Bear, a middle-size present for Mama Bear, and a wee little present for Papa Bear. Baby Bear was very happy.

"Can I open it?" he asked.

"Not till morning," said Mama Bear.

"Morning!" said Santa. "I'd better get going."

The three bears felt the house rumble and shake as Santa went up the chimney and back to his sleigh.

"Sorry about the chair," Santa called. "I'll bring you a new one next year."

And with that, Santa shook the reins and the sleigh took off into the night.